One of a Kind

CHRIS GORMAN

NANCY PAULSEN BOOKS

NANCY PAULSEN BOOKS
an imprint of Penguin Random House LLC
375 Hudson Street
New York, NY 10014

Nancy Paulsen Books is a registered trademark of Penguin Random House LLC.

Library of Congress Cataloging-in-Publication Data is available upon request.

Manufactured in China by RR Donnelley Asia Printing Solutions Ltd.
ISBN 9781524740627
1 3 5 7 9 10 8 6 4 2

Design by Chris Gorman and Marikka Tamura.
The illustrations were created with cameras and computers.

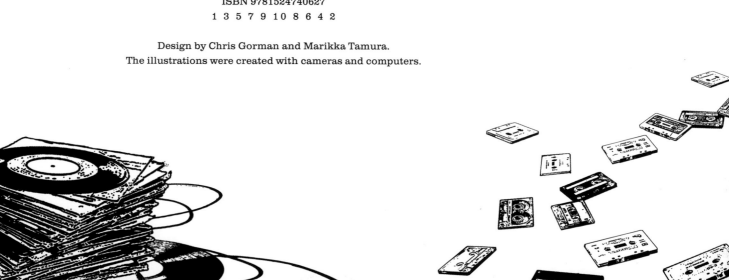

This book is for Toll.

This book would not have been possible without support from
Camille, Claudia, Tom, Jessica and Vicki.
Thank you to Deborah Warren at East/West Literary Agency,
Chad Griffith for photography assistance
and Sharyn Rosart for her encouragement.
Special thanks to Simaiyah Wardana, Marek Raubuck and Indi Gorman
for being in "the band,"
and my own bandmates—Tanya, Gail and Tom.

I'm a kid who's always been a little different.

Maybe it's
the way I dress.

Or the music I like.

It might be
the way I dance!

Or how I *express* myself.

I *like* being

one of a kind.

But *sometimes* **it** **feels** like *something* is *missing.*

It can be *lonely* *and* frustrating!

who *are* a little *different, too,*

to change *things!*

It's *great* to be

one of a *kind*
together.